The Ugly Duckling

CARAMEL TREE

Beautiful Babies

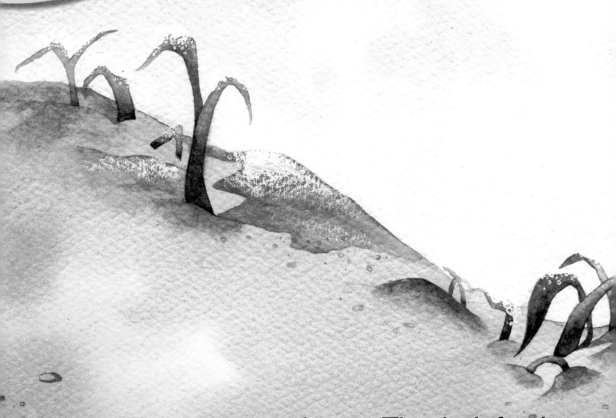

Winter was nearly over. The duck family was looking for a place to nest. They chose Silver Pond. Soon, they had five eggs.

"We will have the most beautiful babies," said Mother Duck.

In spring, four eggs hatched.
Four baby ducklings sat in the nest.
"We have four beautiful babies," said
Father Duck.

Then, the fifth egg hatched.

Mother and Father Duck cried out in surprise.

"What is this?" said Father Duck.

"He is not beautiful like our other babies," said Mother Duck.

The fifth baby had dark gray feathers.
"Ugly Duckling!" said one of the other ducklings.

"But I am beautiful, too!" said Ugly Duckling.

"They are more beautiful than you!" said Father Duck.

What Is Beautiful?

The next day, other birds of Silver Pond came to visit. They saw Ugly Duckling, and they were very surprised.

"You do not look like your sisters," said Seagull. "They are prettier than you."

"You do not look like your brothers," said Crane. "They are more handsome than you."

Ugly Duckling looked at his family. They had smooth white feathers.

He looked at his own feathers. They were different. They were dark and gray.

"What is beautiful?" asked Ugly Duckling.
"We are beautiful," said Mother Duck.
"We have smooth white feathers."

"You are different," said one of the ducklings. "You are ugly."

"I am different," said Ugly Duckling. "I will always be different."

Ugly Duckling walked away. He decided to live alone.

Chapter 3

Alone

Ugly Duckling swam away to the other side of Silver Pond.

He felt sad and alone.

But he never felt angry at anyone. Instead, he always helped them.

When it rained, Ugly Duckling made room in his nest.

When someone was hungry, Ugly Duckling smiled and shared his food.

The summer days passed quickly. Ugly Duckling always made new friends. He helped anyone who needed help. So, he was never alone.

One day, Seagull and Crane came to see Ugly Duckling.

"You should visit your family," said Crane. "You have not seen them all summer."

Ugly Duckling missed his family. "I will visit them soon," he said.

The Kindest and Most Beautiful

Fall brought bright colors to Silver Pond. Everything changed. The leaves on the trees fell off. The green grass changed to golden brown.

Ugly Duckling changed, too. He was not little anymore. But he was still kind.

One day, Ugly Duckling went to visit his family.

"Hello," said Father Duck. "What is your name?"

"I am Ugly Duckling," he said.

"But you are so beautiful!" said Mother Duck.

"I am?" said Ugly Duckling. "What is beautiful?" he asked.

"You have smooth white feathers," said Mother Duck. "You are beautiful!"

"Please come home," said Father Duck.

Ugly Duckling looked at his feathers and smiled. "I can't!" he said. "My friends need me."

"I must go back now. But I will visit you again," he said.

Ugly Duckling said goodbye and swam away. He was the kindest and most beautiful swan on Silver Pond.